The
WITCHES
of
BENEVENTO

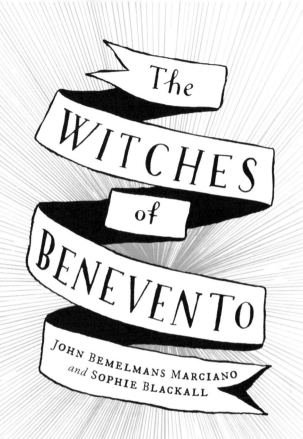

The WITCHES of BENEVENTO

JOHN BEMELMANS MARCIANO
and SOPHIE BLACKALL

RUNAWAY ROSA

A Twins Story

VIKING

VIKING

An imprint of Penguin Random House LLC

375 Hudson Street

New York, New York 10014

First published in the United States of America by Viking,
an imprint of Penguin Random House LLC, 2018

LIBRARY OF CONGRESS CATALOGING-IN-PUBLICATION DATA IS AVAILABLE.
ISBN 9780425291511

1   3   5   7   9   10   8   6   4   2

Manufactured in China   Set in IM FELL French Canon
Book design by Nancy Brennan

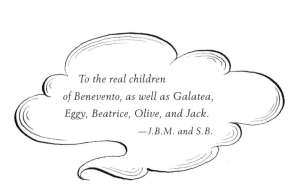

*To the real children
of Benevento, as well as Galatea,
Eggy, Beatrice, Olive, and Jack.*

—J.B.M. and S.B.

Emilio

Rosa

Primo

Maria Beppina

Sergio

CONTENTS

THESE BOOKS ARE LIKE PUZZLES!

LOOK FOR THE FRAMES IN EACH BOOK...

...AND JOIN UP THE PICTURES!

A baby! That's right, a baby! The Twins are about to get a NEW little brother or sister!

There are few events as unforgettable as your mother giving birth. In Benevento, one that comes close is the Hunt of the Boar. But sorry, girls, this contest is just for the boys!

Or _is_ it?

YOUR EVER-FAITHFUL
OBSERVER,
SIGISMONDO
(WITH BRUNO AND RAFAELLA)

RUNAWAY ROSA

A Twins Story

Before we begin . . .

RIGHT now, the Twins and their cousins are at the walled garden of the Crones.

Like a bird, Rosa hops along the high limbs of a tree, plucking apples, not even needing to hold on to any branches for support.

How does she do that? her twin wonders.

Emilio is on the wall, acting as lookout. So he looks out, and he sees their little brother running toward them, screaming.

"There you are!" Dino shouts. "You have to come home! Momma's having the baby! *Momma's having the baby!*"

"I knew it!" Rosa says. "That's why we found that feather!"

This morning, a Janara left a raven's feather on the windowsill—a sign the birth was coming.

"What do you mean, *you* knew it?" Emilio says. "*I* was the one who told you what it meant!"

"Forget all that, guys!" Dino says. "Just COME ON!"

1
BIRTH DAY

AT the Twins' farm, family members and friends are gathered, waiting for Momma to give birth.

At least, the men and kids are waiting—the women are all inside helping.

Outside under the big oak tree, the men play the Game of the Goose, smoke pipes, and drink rosolio. Biscotti are set out on a table nearby.

Well, there *were* biscotti set out, but Rosa and Primo gobbled them all up. Emilio and Maria Beppina each got only one, and nobody saved any for Sergio.

"Where *is* Sergio, anyway?"

"I think one of the Crones got him," Primo says, shrugging while he picks at the last of the crumbs.

"I'm worried about him," Maria Beppina says. "What will they *do* to him?"

Before anyone can answer, their cousin Isidora comes out of the house.

"Is it over?" Primo asks his big sister.

"*No!*" she says, like it was the dumbest question ever asked. "I just came to get Rosa and Maria Beppina."

"What?" Rosa says, scared for once. "Me? Inside *there*? No way!"

Emilio, on the other hand, wishes he could go inside. He's so curious what it's like for a baby to be born.

"What's taking so long in there anyway?" Primo says.

"Don't you know how long it takes to give birth?" Isidora says. "Or how dangerous it is? There's a Cemetery of Dead Babies for a reason."

Isidora shakes her head as she and Maria Beppina go inside the house, leaving Rosa as the only girl outside. Which suits her just fine.

"Hey! Where did all the biscotti go?" Primo's father says.

Rosa and Primo look at each other.

"We've got apples," Primo says, holding out his sack.

Maria Beppina's dad reaches in and takes one. "Where did you get these?" Uncle Tommaso asks.

"Knowing my son, don't ask," Uncle Mimì says, and takes a big loud crunching bite out of one.

The kids get more and more bored. It's been
so hot that the ground is cracked, and Emilio is
poking a stick into a split when Sergio finally
shows up, looking all dusty and with a new hole
in his pants.

"What happened to *you*?" Rosa says.

He shrugs. "That Crone—she caught me! I
couldn't make it up over the wall."

"And then what happened?" Primo says.

"She started talking some crazy stuff. Then she let me go," he says. "It was weird."

"You didn't look her in the eye, did you?" Emilio says.

"No!" Sergio says. "Of course not!" He searches around. "Hey, where are the biscotti?"

"Have an apple," Primo says.

"Hah!" they hear from the circle of men under the oak tree. "A seven! I win!"

It's Primo's poppa, gloating as he moves his piece into the winner's circle. He takes a quattrini from each of the other dads.

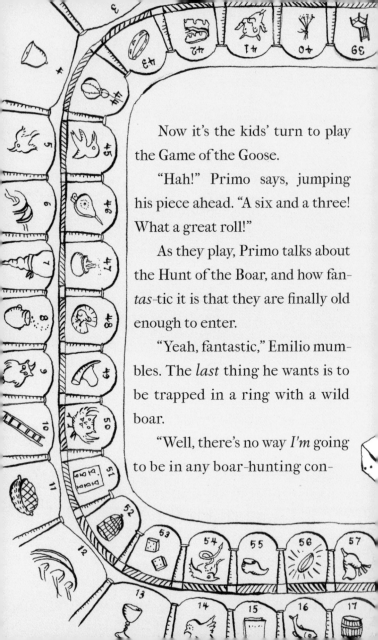

Now it's the kids' turn to play the Game of the Goose.

"Hah!" Primo says, jumping his piece ahead. "A six and a three! What a great roll!"

As they play, Primo talks about the Hunt of the Boar, and how fan-*tas*-tic it is that they are finally old enough to enter.

"Yeah, fantastic," Emilio mumbles. The *last* thing he wants is to be trapped in a ring with a wild boar.

"Well, there's no way *I'm* going to be in any boar-hunting contest," Sergio says, jiggling the dice in the cup. "This is as dangerous a game as I want to be a part of."

He rolls a five, landing him on space thirty-one—the Well. He has to stay trapped there until one of the other players rolls a nine.

"See what I mean?" Sergio says.

They play so many games they get bored of playing, but keep at it anyway. The sun has reached up over the oak tree and is now sinking down the other side. Then they start to hear the moaning.

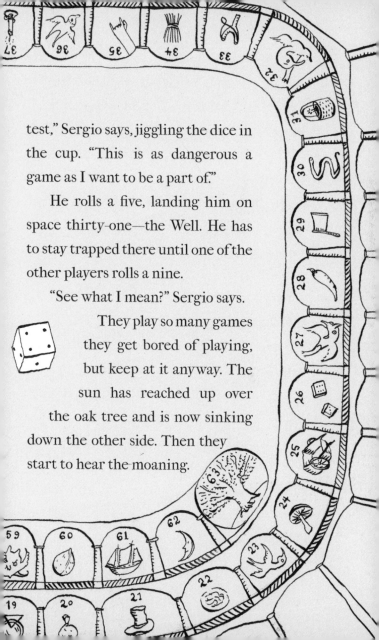

"I know *that* sound," Sergio says to the Twins. "Your mom is having the baby."

Aunt Zufia comes out of the house to fetch Rosa.

"The baby is almost out!" Primo's mom says to her. "Rosa, you have to come or you'll miss it!"

"Noooo way!" Rosa says, shaking her head violently. "I really want to finish this game." She points down to the board with both hands. "I'm winning!"

"No you're not," Primo says. "I am!"

"Can *I* come?" Emilio says.

A look of utter surprise comes to Aunt Zufia's face. "It's really no place for a boy. . . ." she says, but nods for him to come inside anyway.

As Emilio walks in, he feels like he's sneaking, because he doesn't want Father to see.

But Father *does* see, and his pipe practically falls out of his mouth from surprise watching his oldest son enter the birthing room.

Inside, the kitchen feels like the center of the sun, it's so hot and steamy. There is a swirl of activity, and Emilio feels dizzy. He's never seen so many people in their house before! Then he spots Momma.

Maria Beppina is by her head, wiping sweat away from her red, red face. Suddenly, Momma lifts her head up, shuts her eyes tight, and grunts. Then she lays her head back down.

"That's the pushing, Emilio," Aunt Zufia whispers. "Look—you can see the head of the baby!"

After a few more minutes of his mom pushing, the baby is all the way out.

Aunt Zufia and Sergio's mom take the baby to wash it and Emilio goes to Momma.

"Are you okay?" he says.

She smiles, seeing him there. "I'm wonderful!" she says, and takes his hand.

He smiles too.

Sergio's mother hands Momma the baby, all packaged up in a white-and-blue-checked towel. Its purply-red face is the only thing sticking out. Isidora, Maria Beppina, and all the women gather around to see.

"Is it a boy or a girl?" Emilio asks Momma.

"Why don't you look for yourself?"

A little embarrassed, he does just that.

"Why don't you go out and tell them, dear?" Momma says.

Emilio opens the door into what now seems like a cool spring breeze.

All the men and boys freeze in what they are doing—game-playing, drinking, smoking, eating—and look at him.

"It's a GIRL!" Emilio says.

And everybody cheers.

2

ROSA'S LAST STAND

THREE days later, all the ladies who have been helping out are gone, and Momma is back on her feet.

After breakfast, Poppa and the kids head out to work like normal. But then Momma calls Rosa to stay in the kitchen.

Rosa stands there frozen, desperate to leave. She's been avoiding Momma and the baby like the plague.

"Do you want to hold her?" Momma says, offering the baby.

"Why would I want to *hold* it?!" Rosa says.

When she does hold her—again reluctantly—the baby starts to cry.

"See? She doesn't want me holding her either!"

"She's just hungry," Momma says, and begins to nurse her.

Rosa looks away.

"Listen, dear," Momma says. "I want to talk to you about something. . . ."

Gently, she tells Rosa that Dino is now old enough to help Emilio and Poppa with everything that needs doing around the farm. "And *I* need *your* help taking care of the baby. Not to mention all the other house chores—cooking, cleaning, clothes-making . . ."

"WHAT?" Rosa is flabbergasted by the suggestion. "*WHAT?*"

"Things have changed," Momma says.

"Why does *anything* have to change?!"

Rosa can't understand it—why should *she* have to help with the stupid baby? Why not Emilio? Rosa is furious and outraged at the injustice of it all and "I won't do it! I just **WON'T!**"

Momma says that she and Father have talked and it's already been decided.

"And it will be nice to have you inside the house."

"It's *not* nice," Rosa says. "It's prison. *Baby* prison!" And she stomps off.

At the stand, Primo thinks the news is the funniest thing he's ever heard.

"Rosa the maid! Hah-hah!"

Rosa punches him in the shoulder.

The worst part is that Rosa won't be allowed to take the cart into town in the morning anymore.

"This is my **last** trip!"

Emilio thinks it isn't fair either.

Primo, on the other hand, doesn't seem to care at all.

As they talk, Sergio's stepdad comes into the piazza, blows his trumpet, and cries out the news. At the end, he mentions the Hunt of the

Boar. It's happening in ten days, and the sign-up for contestants will happen Sunday after church.

"All boys in their tenth year are eligible!" he cries. "Come make your mark!"

Primo is ecstatic. It's all he's been talking about—not just lately, but for forever!

"Aren't you excited, Emilio?" Primo says. "We can sign up together!"

Emilio shrinks. *Everyone* expects him to sign up, which makes him not wanting to all the worse.

Rosa says she is entering too, and Primo laughs at her. "Hah! *Girls* can't do it!"

JUST WATCH ME, DONKEY BRAINS!

"Just watch me, donkey brains!"

The next stop with Ugo and the cart is Sergio's house, to drop off a basket of eggs. His ghost is their single best egg customer.

Rosa knocks on the door. Sergio opens it and says, "Yeah? What?"

It's weird. He says it like he doesn't even know her.

"Here are your eggs," Rosa says.

Sergio looks down at them and scrunches up his nose in a way she's never seen him do before. "Why would I want all those?"

"They're not for you, donkey brains!" Rosa says. "They're for your *ghost*!"

"My *what*?" he says, nose scrunching again. "Oh right, her."

"*Her?*"

Sergio mumbles something, grabs the eggs, and shuts the door.

Rosa walks back to the cart. Maria Beppina has come down and is talking to Emilio.

"That's it," Rosa says to them. "Sergio's finally lost his marbles!"

"You noticed it too?" Maria Beppina says. "He's been acting so strange the last few days."

Heading back upstairs, she turns and waves goodbye. "See you tomorrow," she says to Emilio.

Rosa pulls herself up to the seat next to her twin. "What are you guys doing tomorrow?"

"Nothing!" Emilio says.

"What nothing?" Rosa says, squinting. "Are you hiding secrets again?"

"What? No way!"

But he is.

3

DAY ONE OF THE REST
OF YOUR LIFE

THE next morning, Ugo pulls the cart down the lane and turns onto the road into town. Emilio doesn't even need to touch the reins. The ox treads the same path every day and knows the way himself. But this isn't just another day.

Emilio turns around and sees Rosa still standing where they left her. She's watching them leave, with the saddest, most forlorn look Emilio has ever seen his twin have.

"I feel bad for her," he says.

"Well, I don't!" Dino says, thrilled to be in the front seat. "That's what she gets for beating me up all the time!"

"Rosa!" Momma calls from inside the house. "Rosa! I need your help. Right **now**!"

Rosa looks over to Poppa, who is fixing the fence. He pulls down an eyelid.

She sighs with all her body and walks into the house.

This is the worst day ever.

Momma tells Rosa everything that needs to be done in the kitchen, but Rosa is managing to learn none of it.

"It's like you're *trying* not to pay attention!" Momma says, exasperated with her.

But how can she pay attention wearing this *stupid* new head scarf? It's the size of a towel!

"Now this is very important," Momma says, and tells her about Foca, the sprite of the hearth. "Foca has lived in our chimney for hundreds of years. She's old and cranky, but if you make the right offering every morning she'll make anything you do a little bit easier, and all the food taste a little bit better."

Momma tells Rosa to crumble one leaf of
sage into the fire, and when it flares, say:

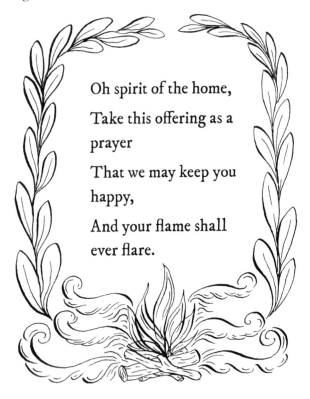

Oh spirit of the home,
Take this offering as a
prayer
That we may keep you
happy,
And your flame shall
ever flare.

But Rosa can't say it without screwing up.

"Will you at least please *try*, Rosa?" Momma
says.

"But it's so hard to remember!"

Next she has to wipe the morning plates.

"Why should *I* have to clean my brothers' dirty plates?"

"Someone's been doing it for *you* all these years," Momma says. "While the men are *out* working we are *in* working. A family has roles."

"But I don't want *this* role! I want *that* role!" Rosa says, pointing outside.

Momma smiles at her— that pitying parent smile.

"Let's try something fun," she says. "The best way to carry heavy things is on your head. Let's practice with this basket of napkins."

Momma does a perfect demonstration, walking across the room without

once lifting a hand to help balance the basket, while holding the baby to boot.

"Now *you* try."

Rosa takes one step and the basket goes *drop*. Back on the head, *drop*. And again—*drop*.

Momma can only shake her head.

"Is it time for lunch yet?" Rosa says.

"*Lunch?*" Momma says. "The third hour bell hasn't even rung yet!"

"But the summer hours are so *lo-o-ong!*" Rosa whines.

Up at the vegetable stand, Primo looks surprised to see Dino in Rosa's seat.

"Where's Rosa?" he says.

"We *told* you she has to stay home with the baby from now on," Emilio says.

Dino smiles.

"Hah! No more Rosa!" Primo says. "That's great." But the look on his face doesn't seem like he thinks it's so great.

Back home, the parade of indignities continues. The worst of it is lunch, formerly Rosa's favorite event of the day—of life itself.

With the baby napping, Momma begins a soup, but Rosa drops a pan—**CLANK!**—and the baby wakes up crying, and Rosa has to finish making the soup.

Not only does she have to fix lunch, though. Rosa has to *serve* her brothers.

"This is so great!" Dino says, hardly able to believe what is happening.

Rosa slugs him in the shoulder. And not like she usually does, but hard.

Dino bursts into tears.

Momma gets mad at Rosa for hitting her brother; Father gets mad at Dino for crying.

Emilio, meanwhile, takes a taste of the soup and makes a face.

"I think there's something wrong with this," he says.

"Your sister made it," Momma says. "And I think it's very good."

She says this, however, before she samples it. Once she does, she has to force a smile. And gulp the food down.

After lunch, Momma takes pity on Rosa and lets her go into town on an errand—to borrow diapers from Sergio's mom.

Even though she's finally getting to leave the kitchen, the fact that Rosa is getting *diapers* keeps it from being fun. She's *never* going to have babies!

Rosa is so hopping mad about the injustice of it all she forgets to make the horns and spit going through the walls. Malefix, the spirit of the arch, trips her. She falls to the ground and the spirit laughs. The sound of it echoes like there are *three* spirits laughing.

"You dirty rotten sprite!" Rosa says, getting up and shaking her fist at him.

The worst insult you can give a spirit is to call them a sprite, but it doesn't bother Malefix.

You dirty rotten sprite! You dirty rotten sprite! the mocking echo of Malefix shouts back.

"Ah, you're the *least* of my worries today!" Rosa says, and gives him the peck with her hand and elbow.

You're the least of my worries today! You're the least of my worries today!

The voice of Malefix follows her, even when she's really too far away to hear it anymore.

4

THE A-B-C-DARIAN

HIS family thinks he is going off to pick mush-rooms.

He is not.

Instead he is going off to do something *no* one in his family has ever done before. Something unspeakable.

If Poppa ever finds out about it, Emilio will get into the biggest trouble of his life. *Rosa*-sized trouble.

Emilio is learning how to **read**.

For the last month, he has been sneaking off every afternoon to see Maria Beppina, who is teaching him from an ABC primer.

Reading is both forbidden and dangerous. The reason is that Father—like most folks they know—believes books are either the work of evil sorcerers or for starting revolutions or just plain *nonsense* and that nothing good has ever come from one.

Emilio is so afraid of getting caught that he's jumpy. Outside of Maria Beppina's house, he peers around to make sure no one sees him before climbing her stairs. Which is why he practically leaps out of his skin when he hears:

"**Boy**!"

It's Amerigo Pegleg, calling so loudly anyone can hear.

"Are you excited to enter the big contest, boy?" he says. "The Hunt of the Boar!"

Does everyone have to keep asking him that?

Amerigo goes on about how *he* won the Golden Tusk when he was a boy. He sounds just like Father.

Then the old soldier lowers his voice.

"Did you know that Janara watch the Boar Hunt with intense interest? They can even help those they favor." He winks and says, "You know, *Janara?*"

Amerigo hasn't mentioned the Janara since he told Emilio that he used to be one—and that someone Emilio knows is a Janara *now*.

"So have ye figured it out yet, boy?" he says, leaning in with his hot horrible breath. "Or should I say *who?*"

Emilo shakes his head no.

"I'm surprised, a smart boy like you, and what with this person not being so . . ." Amerigo clucks his tongue against the roof of his mouth. "Not so very *careful.*"

The old soldier chuckles and rocks himself on down the street.

Emilio quickly dashes up the steps before anyone else sees him.

"Is your dad here?" he says to Maria Beppina when he walks in. She shakes her head no.

Not that it matters. Her dad is the one and only person who *can* know what he's doing. In fact, Uncle Tommaso is thrilled that Emilio wants to learn how to read, and has promised not to breathe a word of it to any other parent.

They get right down to the lesson.

Today, Maria Beppina is explaining how certain letters change sound in front of other letters, like a *c* or *g* in front of an *i* or *e*.

"Why would they do *that*?" he says. "It's not logical."

"They just do," Maria Beppina says. Then she has him read some example sentences and Emilio keeps mixing up the hard *c*'s and *g*'s with the soft *c*'s and *g*'s. He gets more and more frustrated, and now his head is starting to hurt.

"I can't do it!" Emilio finally says. "I'm not smart enough!"

A look of pure shock comes to Maria Beppina's face.

"How can you *say* that?" she says. "You're the smartest kid in town!"

"Not with reading," he says.

"But it's *hard* to learn how to read," she says.

"So how come you and your dad can do it so easily?"

"It only gets easy later. Everything is hard at first, right?"

Emilio isn't sure about that. Nothing he's ever tried was half as hard as this.

"How about we practice writing the alphabet?" Maria Beppina says, and they go over to her father's drawing table. She opens the inkwell and hands Emilio a pen.

"No, I've got one," he says, taking a fresh hawk feather out of one of his pockets. He cuts off the end and *presto!* A new pen.

He dips the pen in the ink and starts, **A . . . B . . . C . . .**

Suddenly, the door flips open.

It's Sergio.

Oh, no!

"What are you guys doing?" he says.

Emilio quickly puts the pen down.

"You know how to WRITE, farmboy?" Sergio says.

Which is a really odd thing for him to say. Why would he be insulting Emilio like that?

"I'm just drawing pictures," Emilio mumbles.

"Of the letters A-B-C!" Sergio says.

Emilio crumples the paper.

"How do *you* know how to read those letters?" Maria Beppina says.

"Well, er, I don't!" he says. "I mean, I just know those three. Who *doesn't* know those three?"

"Pretty much everyone," Emilio says.

Emilio and Maria Beppina look at each other. Why is Sergio acting so *weird*?

"This is boring! Let's go swimming down at the river!" Sergio says. "I haven't gone swimming in *years*!"

Which is the weirdest thing Sergio has said yet.

"When did Sergio ever want to go into the river unless he *had* to?" Maria Beppina whispers to Emilio as they follow Sergio out. "He's terrified of Manalonga! And what does he mean by *years*?"

But Emilio isn't worried about Sergio acting weird—he's worried about Sergio telling someone what he just saw!

"Look, we have to be more careful about this," Emilio says. "Let's go to the woods tomorrow. That way I can pick mushrooms too."

They make a plan to meet outside the Inn at the Fork at the sixth hour bell. Up ahead, Sergio turns the corner and starts yelling.

Then they turn the corner too and see exactly what he is yelling at.

One of the Crones!

She has a look of **fury** in her eyes!

"Run! Run! She knows it was us in the garden!" Sergio shouts, pushing them back the other way. "Don't look into her eyes! Don't listen to what she says! She's come for her revenge! She'll melt your face!"

"No, *wait*!" the Crone shouts.

But whatever she has to say, Emilio doesn't want to hear it!

5

ROSA OF THE TREES

THE first time Rosa wakes up, it's because of the crying. It's so loud it sounds like it's *inside* her head.

"Rosa," Momma says, handing her the hysterical infant. "I've been up all night. I need you to walk the baby back to sleep."

"*Whaaat?*" Rosa says, bleary-eyed and unable to believe her mother could suggest such a thing. "It's still dark out!"

Rosa winds up back asleep with the baby on top of her.

The next time Rosa wakes up it is because of the feeling of someting wet on her.

Spit-up.

"SKEEV-O!" she says, and takes the baby back to Momma.

The third time she wakes it's because of her mother shaking her.

"Come on, Rosa!" Momma says. "You have to help with breakfast!"

Her brothers and father are already at the table waiting and when no one else is looking she sticks her tongue out at Dino.

Momma, meanwhile, is making food.

"Here," she says, and hands Rosa the baby. The baby isn't even wearing a diaper. Which is a bad thing.

Rosa feels something wet on her again. And warm.

This time it's pee.

I QUIT!

"That's *it*!" Rosa says, handing Emilio the baby. "I quit!"

"You can't quit!" Momma says.

"Just watch me!" Rosa says. "And I don't just quit this baby—I quit this whole *family*!"

Rosa throws open the shutters, climbs up onto the window ledge, grabs the limb of the big oak tree outside, and swings herself up into the tree. She then leans back down.

"From now on, I live in the trees!" she says, making a vow with raised arm. "My feet will never touch the ground again!"

Her father pulls down an eyelid.

And then Rosa does the unthinkable.

She pulls down an eyelid *back* at him.

Father's face
goes **red**, but Rosa
is already gone in a
rustle of leaves.

"Should I go get her?"
Emilio says.

Momma shakes her head no. "Let her
be. Besides, how could you ever catch her?"

Emilio and Dino take the cart into town. As
Ugo turns onto the road, Emilio gets hit in the
back of the neck with something. It stings.

An olive falls to the floor of the cart.

The brothers look back to see Rosa in the
olive orchard, laughing. Before she can launch
more olives from her slingshot, Emilio shakes
the reins and hurries Ugo toward town.

Free! Rosa thinks. *I'm free!*

She'll never again have to do anything anyone tells her to do. And no more taking care of

babies and
serving little
brothers, either!

Rosa hops tree to
tree until she herself reaches
the main road, which is lined
with oaks and chestnuts all the way
to the river. Well, almost all the way to
the river.

Between the tree she is in and the tree next to the bridge is a wide-open space—it's got to be at least twenty feet. Way too far to jump.

Rosa looks around. There's no one to see her, so no one to catch her if she cheats a little.

She jumps down and leaps her longest steps—one, two, three, four, five!—and is fast back up a tree.

Rosa decides to make a five-step rule. It's okay to take five steps out of a tree if it's to get to another tree.

After playing near the river, Rosa wants to go into town. However, the only way to cross the water is the bridge.

Do bridges count as ground? Probably, she thinks, but decides the *side* wall of the bridge is okay.

She walks on it with her arms out in a T for balance.

Rosa! Hey, Rosa! she hears from under the bridge. *It's*

*me, Primo! Hey, you can't believe what I found under here! It's a bottle! And inside of it is a house! And inside of the house are tiny little people, and they're WAVING at me! Come on and just lean over a **tiny** bit more. . . .*

"Pipe down, you dirty rotten Manalonga!" Rosa yells. "I've got important things to do!"

ROSA! HEY, ROSA!

Reaching the fork, who does Rosa see driving along but her brothers, with Primo riding in the back.

Up in her tree, she keeps as still as she can until the cart is passing just underneath. Then she shouts:

"Hey, **donkey brains**! Why are you in the back? Did your dad trade you for a bag of tomatoes?"

Startled, Primo jumps, and Rosa laughs.

"So it's true," Primo says. "You *have* done the stupidest thing ever. You went to live in the trees."

"Yes I did," Rosa says. "And it's *not* stupid! From this day forward, I am the Queen of the Trees!"

"More like the Farmgirl of the Bushes," Primo says.

Rosa makes the marameo at him and leaps away.

All the boys can do is brush off the leaves falling on their heads.

Right now, Rosa is *really* hungry. Why didn't she bring food up here?

And it gets boring living in the trees a lot more quickly than you'd think. They aren't really comfortable for napping, either, although Rosa does manage to take a pretty long one.

When she wakes up, Rosa goes into town. There are so few trees there she has to come up with a new rule: She doesn't have to be in a tree at *all* times, she just can't ever set foot on the ground. (Except for the five-step rule.)

This new rule lets her circle the Trig-

gio across the city walls and rooftops to get where she needs to go. The Theater.

Inside the Theater, she finds Maria Beppina and Isidora at the tailor's where they are making costumes for the pageant, which is the play that happens right before the Hunt of the Boar.

Perched on the tile roof of the tailor's, Rosa begs Isidora for a chunk of sausage and some dried figs.

She and Isidora have lunch together—even if it's from different heights—while Maria Beppina goes home to eat with her dad.

At least that's what she *said*.

When Rosa climbs back up the walls of the Theater, however, she sees that Maria Beppina isn't going home. In fact, she is headed the other way—*out* of town.

From above, Rosa follows her all the way out of the city. At the Inn at the Fork, she sees that Maria Beppina is meeting someone. Emilio!

What are those two up to?

Rosa thinks that maybe it has something to do with what they were whispering to each other yesterday.

Emilio and Maria Beppina head into the woods. There are plenty of leafy trees so it's easy for Rosa to tail them without being seen.

At a small clearing by a stream, her brother and cousin sit on a rock side by side and lean their heads toward one another.

Rosa can't believe it!

"*SKEEV-O*!" she yells. "Are you guys **KISS-ING**?!"

The two of them jump up and practically fall off the rock.

"What! *Kissing?*" Emilio says. "No! No way!

"We're just reading!" Maria Beppina says, holding up the book.

"*Reading?*" Rosa says, squinting. "That's even worse! And since when do you know how to read, donkey brains?"

"I'm trying to learn," Emilio says, red-faced.

"You are going to get in *trouble*!" Rosa says.

"**Please** don't tell Poppa!" Emilio says.

"If I did he'd kill you! Imagine! Perfect Emilio getting into trouble!" Rosa smiles at the thought of it. Then she shrugs it away. "But I'm not going to. You know why? Because I'm not even a member of your family anymore. I'm the Queen of the Trees!"

With a loud whoop she scares a flock of birds into the sky and disappears somewhere into the forest.

Bong bong, BONG bong!

When she hears the evening bell, Rosa's heart leaps with the thought that it's dinner time. But . . . not for her.

Sigh.

Her stomach grumbles.

What is Momma making for supper? Rosa wonders. She's so curious she can't help herself from tree-hopping all the way back home.

Before she even reaches the oak beside the kitchen window she can smell it—*scamorza alla griglia!* Roasted cheese! Her favorite thing in the entire world!

How can life be so cruel?

Rosa sits in the tree just outside the window, trying to hide herself in the leaves as she watches her former family eat. Her heart sinks as Dino asks for seconds. There isn't anything left on the platter now. But then she sees it—a plate set out in her place, with a perfect slab of golden-crusted scamorza just lying on it.

Emilio hears a rustle, looks up, and sees his twin. He can't tell if their parents see her, too.

He goes back to looking down at his plate. Everyone just focuses on their food, not saying a word, and keeps doing so as Rosa quietly climbs down to the windowsill, slips inside the house, takes her seat on the bench, and starts to eat.

6

PUT YOUR X HERE

THE only thing that makes Rosa's situation any less awful than it was before she went into the trees is the fact that she now can hold Emilio's secret against him. Rosa threatens to tell Father about his reading unless her twin helps her change diapers.

(Which Emilio doesn't even mind, but lets her *think* he hates doing.)

The worst day yet, however, is Sunday. Isn't it supposed to be the day of rest? But there *isn't* any rest, not when you're taking care of a baby!

Dumb baby.

However, having to take care of a baby in church winds up not being such a bad thing.

Usually, Rosa snoozes through church—the service is in *Latin*, after all—but Momma makes her hold the baby, so she can't. Then the baby starts crying—really **LOUDLY**—and people around them start shifting in their seats uncomfortably and Momma tells Rosa to take the baby outside.

Rosa doesn't need to be told twice!

"I guess you don't like Latin, either!" she says to the baby as they wait on the steps outside. Church lets out and now everyone is hanging around the steps when Sergio's stepdad arrives. He announces that this is the offical sign-up for the Great Hunt of the Boar.

"Any boy in his tenth year may now step up and make his mark!"

The hunt occurs once a year, when the entrances to the Theater are blocked up and a wild boar is let loose to run amok in the old arena. The contestants dress up in ancient-looking costumes with strap-up sandals and vie to win the Golden Tusk, the trophy awarded to whoever catches the boar. Participating is a rite of passage in the Triggio, and all the dads talk about when *they* were in the contest.

Primo and Mozzo push and jostle each other out of the way to be the first to sign up.

Emilio groans. He wishes he could disappear.

"Come on, Emilio!" Primo says after he signs. "Make your mark!"

"Maybe he's too chicken!" Mozzo says.

The attention is taken off Emilio for the moment by the next boy to step forward.

Sergio!

Sergio? Didn't he just say he'd never join the boar hunt?

His stepdad pulls the sheet away from him.

"Are you *sure* you want to do this?" he says, a look of concern on his face.

"Yes!" Sergio says. "Now give it!"

"My little boy," Sergio's mom says, beaming as he makes his X. "Finally becoming a man!"

Now Emilio feels even more pressure to sign up!

"Come *on*, chicken! What are you waiting for?" Mozzo says.

Emilio looks over to Poppa. He knows his father wants nothing more than to have a son win the Golden Tusk, just like he did.

Now *everyone* is looking at Emilio. All the boys his age have signed up except him.

"Here, I'll even get the pen ready for you," Mozzo says, dipping the quill into the ink and holding it out for him.

Emilio wants to be writing A-B-C's, not X's. "Bawk-bawk-*baaawk*!"

"You can't let Mozzo make fun of you like that!" Primo says. "Come on, show him what you're made of, Emilio. Sign it!"

"Yeah, sign it!" Sergio says.

Emilio looks at the faces of all the people. Of his father. And then at the pen.

A drop of ink rolls off the tip and makes a splat on the ground.

"Ah, he's not gonna sign up," Rosa says, pulling the quill out of Mozzo's hand. "But **I** am!"

She makes a big fat **X** right at the bottom of the sheet.

"Hey, she can't do that!" Mozzo says. "No girls allowed!"

"Yeah, that's right!" Primo says. He turns

to Sergio's stepdad. "Isn't that right?"

The crier reads back over the rules and shrugs. "It doesn't say here that only boys can enter."

"I'm not just entering the contest," Rosa says. "I'm going to *win* it."

There is a big loud "Hah!"

It's not from Mozzo, or from Primo either.

It's from Father.

He has a horrible grinning smirk on his face that makes Rosa furious.

"You shouldn't be laughing! *I* may be the best son you'll ever have!" Rosa says. "Emilio is too scared to even enter!"

"Am not!" Emilio says. "I just don't *want* to!"

Everyone starts to argue.

Momma tries to calm them down, and also to stop Rosa from entering the contest.

"It's too dangerous!" she says. "When I was your age, a boy got gored by the boar's tusks and almost died!"

"Well, I ain't no **boy**," Rosa says, and hands the pen back to Sergio's stepdad.

Father shakes his head. "You'll never win."

It is about the most he has ever said.

"Oh yeah?" she says. "Well, if you're so sure, then how about we make a bet? If I *do* win, then I get to go back to working in the fields and making the deliveries in town—no more baby prison! But if I *lose*, then I'll keep helping in the house and never complain again!"

Now Father smiles a big wide smile and nods his head yes. To seal the deal, they grab pinkies, hold a hand over their hearts, and spit—the unbreakable triple-swear.

Emilio breathes a sigh of relief. At least no one is paying attention to *him* anymore.

7

HOW TO CATCH A WILD BOAR

FATHER is furious at Emilio. He can't understand why any boy would not want to enter the Boar Hunt. And what Rosa said only made things worse.

Which is why Emilio can't believe it when Rosa asks him to help her.

"Why should I help *you*?" he says.

"Why shouldn't you?"

"Because of what you said to Father," Emilio says. "That *you're* the best son he'll ever have!"

"Ah, phooey!" she says. "Forget about that."

Rosa keeps pushing until finally Emilio says, "Fine! I'll do it. But then we're *even*! You never tell Father about my learning how to read, and I don't have to keep helping you with the baby."

Even though he still doesn't mind it. But it's the principle of the thing.

To seal the deal, the Twins triple-swear on it.

As for *how* Emilio can help Rosa, he has a few ways.

First off, he knows a lot about boars. When it's truffle season, he follows them through the woods until they start digging and then snatches the prized mushrooms away from them. He tells Rosa how to sneak up on them and— more importantly— how to make them afraid of you.

Secondly, he teaches Rosa knots. Specifically, how to quickly lasso and hogtie a boar. After he demonstrates, Rosa hands him the baby and tries for herself.

As usual, Rosa gets frustrated quickly—although not as frustrated as their poor hog, Ivan, whom she is practicing on. Soon enough, however, she can tie him up as fast as you can count to three.

Next—and most importantly—there's strategy. Emilio may have no desire to participate in the Boar Hunt, but he loves *watching* it and knows all the winners and how they did it.

"Whoever goes first always loses. You want to be the last one to go—let the others tire the boar out. That's the secret to why the Carrozzos win. So whatever you do, be patient and don't let Mozzo goad you into going before him." Two things that will not be easy for Rosa.

The final thing is to go to the Theater itself,

to look at where the hunt actually happens.

When they get there, they find Primo's and Maria Beppina's fathers hard at work on the pageant. Uncle Mimì is finishing building the stage while Uncle Tommaso paints the backdrop. Isidora and Maria Beppina are there, too, working on the costumes they've been making with the tailor.

"Wow, Uncle Tommaso," Emilio says, watching him paint. "You're really good!"

"Thank you!" he says enthusiastically. "Isn't this wonderful? The Theater used *just* as the Romans intended—for a drama!"

"We know, we know!" the others all say in unison.

In the corner of his mouth, Primo's poppa holds three nails, which he hammers down with loud bangs.

"SO!" he says to Rosa. "I hear you've entered the contest for the Golden Tusk!"

"Yes, sir!" she says.

"Well, I for one hope you win!" Then he

whispers to her, *"In fact, I'm betting on it!"* And winks.

"You know, it was a woman who won the original hunt for the wild boar—the Calydonian boar!" Uncle Tommaso says. "All the greatest heroes of Ancient Greece gathered to see who could kill the rampaging giant beast, and the winner was Atalanta, the lone woman."

"Isidora!" Maria Beppina says excitedly to their eldest cousin "We have to make Rosa an Atalanta costume for the hunt!"

Isidora agrees, and Rosa goes with them to

get fitted for a costume, while Emilio heads home. He's relieved that Maria Beppina has been too busy with the costumes to help him read lately. It was getting so frustrating.

When he's feeling down, Emilio likes to go to the upper part of the city and look in the open windows of the fancy shops. As he walks, he passes Zì Filippo, stirring his pot of wax, and looks at the sign above his head:

"Candles," Emilio says, looking at the letters. "*Candles!*"

Emilio has passed that sign a thousand times and it was always just a jumble of symbols. But now he can **read** it. It's like MAGIC!

He's so excited that he starts walking around town, just *looking* for signs.

"*Butcher!*" he reads.

"*Salt and Tobacco!*"

"*Shoemaker!*"

CARRIAGES

SALT

"Carriages for hire!"

Oh, words never sound so good as when you're *reading* them! He breaks off into a run, just to get more words—*Baker! Hatmaker! Baker* again!

He's stuck in a dizzy, dreamy, swirling world of words. Which is why he bumps into Amerigo Pegleg, almost knocking him over.

"I'm so sorry, Zì Amerigo!" Emilio says, grabbing the old soldier's arm to help steady him. "I didn't see you!"

"That's quite all right, my boy. **Quite** all right!" Amergio adjusts his tricorn hat with a big smile. "Nothing in the world could bother me today!"

Amerigo starts to pick small flowers growing in the cracks of the buildings and whistles a short happy tune.

"I tell you, boy, I haven't been this happy since Yorktown! That's when we won the Revolution, you know!" He chuckles. "Now, don't ask me *why* I'm so happy, because I couldn't tell you even if I wanted to!" He leans in, with that aw-

ful breath of his. "I will tell you it's about a *lady*, however!"

He lets out another chuckle of delight, gives a spin on his leg, and carries his growing bouquet up the street.

Adults are so strange!

8

THE HUNT

EMILIO has never seen his twin care about what she is wearing before. But today she's fussing over every single item.

"How does the skirt look?" Rosa says. "Should I have the belt high, or low?"

But today is not any other today. Today is the Hunt of the Wild Boar!

"You look great. Like a real Amazon," Emilio says. "Can we *go* now?"

As the whole family walks into town, Rosa can't contain herself. She's less walking than skip-hopping there.

In through the city walls—horns and *spit*!—

the streets of the Triggio are already buzzing with excitement.

On the steps of the church, the kids in their costumes are assembling.

Contestants go in back! Little kids in the middle! Musicians up front!

Then the wild boar makes its appearance and everyone gathers around the cage to see.

"It's a big one this year!"

"HUGE!"

"Ah, I've seen bigger."

Everyone has an opinion.

The boar is on a kind of stretcher called a litter, which is carried by the Order of the Golden Tusk—the winners of contests past. At the front is Pozzo Carrozzo, who wears the golden sash of the reigning champion.

"In a few hours it's gonna be *me* wearing that gold belt!" Primo says.

"No way!" Mozzo says. "That's practically a piece of our family wardrobe, we've won it so many times!"

Rosa is about to pipe in when Emilio cuts her off.

"For one day in your life, be patient," he says. "Good luck!"

Dino takes his place with the other young boys, all holding spears. The small girls are wearing garlands of vines in their hair and holding baskets of flowers.

Suddenly, the drum!

baRUMPumPUM!

Everyone's heart leaps.

baRUMPumPUM!

Now the zampogna hums its deep throaty song while the flute adds a tune that floats like a bird skipping around the sky.

The crowd cheers as the little girls throw flowers and the younger boys poke the air with their spears, and at last the contestants start to march! Rosa can't help but smile—the kind of smile that hurts your face.

Then she feels an elbow to her ribs. Mozzo!

"You don't belong here!"

Before Rosa can speak, Sergio says, "You shut your beak, you little turd!"

"Thanks, Sergio!" Rosa yells above the noise.

"*We girls have to stick together!*" Sergio says. Or at least, that's what Rosa *thinks* he said.

"*What* did you just say?"

"We cousins have to stick together!" he says. Which makes a lot more sense.

MOZZO   FORTUNATO   BARDO   PRIMO   SER

The parade winds its way up through the Triggio and into the arch between Zia Pia's house and Amerigo Pegleg's hovel. As they enter the Theater the crowd *roars*!

The ancient arena is PACKED with people, crammed into every nook and cranny—on the old Roman seats and steps, inside the houses and workshops, and on the rooftops.

Everyone they know is here, and many they don't. This is the one day of the year

ROSA

FONZO

CERUZZO

BIASO

LITTLE EFI

when the Triggio is visited by people from the fancy part of town—up where they have paved roads and glass windows and everyone wears shoes.

Now comes the pageant. Rosa can never sit still for one of these things! And *then* there's a long boring speech by some town official.

"The Hunt of the Boar is not just a game," he says. "Rather, it is a contest of strength, of speed, and of smarts!"

"Well, you have two out of three," Primo whispers to Rosa.

Punch.

"And now," the official says. "It's time!"

pruPROO!

The Town Crier blows his horn, explains the rules, and calls the contestants forward. Primo volunteers to go first and Sergio's step-dad again sounds his horn. The boar is released. The hunt is **on**!

Perched atop the tailor's along-side his girl-cousins, Emilio has a perfect view of the action. Primo does absolutely everything Emilio told Rosa *not* to do. He races around, now chasing, now being chased by the boar. Primo falls and gets up so much that the crowd starts to laugh, and it's a relief when the horn sounds, ending his turn.

Next go the brick- and barrel-makers' sons, who don't do much better. The boar isn't anywhere close to tuckered out yet, and both of them get chased more than they do any chasing.

Now comes Little Efi, the son of the blacksmith. Despite his name, he's the biggest kid their age and as strong as the horses he helps his dad to shoe. He could wrestle the boar down with his bare hands, which even the animal seems to undersand. The boar runs away from 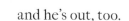 him and Little Efi is too slow to catch it. The horn blares and he's out, too.

Sergio goes next. When they were wrestling the other day, Sergio got Emilio into a headlock and wouldn't let go until Rosa pulled him off. The new Sergio isn't only brave and strong, he's *mean*.

But not that smart when it comes to boars.

He charges straight at it and **Pow**! The boar rams him with a tusk, lifting his feet right up off the ground. Sergio lands on the ground— *thud!*—like a sack of grain.

OUCH!

A whole gaggle of people run into the arena from behind the barriers to attend to Sergio and keep the boar at bay.

"I'm fine, I'm fine!" Sergio hollers. "It's just a scratch!"

But it's more than that. He gets carried out of

the arena, with his mother and Maria Beppina following. Emilio thinks maybe he should go, too, but he has to wait for Rosa to have her turn.

Rosa, meanwhile, is thinking to herself, *Do NOT run straight at the boar.*

When the action gets started again, it's the turn of Tonino, the tanner's kid. After seeing what just happened, he stays as far away from the boar as he can. The next few boys seem to be thinking the same thing, and now there are only two contestants left: Rosa and Mozzo.

"Ladies first," Mozzo says, extending his arm.

"Ah, you're just scared and hoping *I* win so you don't have to get in the ring!" Rosa says.

She makes Mozzo so furious that he *insists* on going next.

Rosa looks for Emilio in the crowd and winks at him.

What she can't hear is Emilio yelling for her to "Go next! Go *next!*" The boar is breathing hard and totally exhausted.

Emilio's heart sinks as he watches Mozzo enter the arena.

Mozzo stalks the boar for a few steps, then manages to pin its hip against a barrel. The boar can't charge forward or back up. Mozzo takes out his loop of rope and goes to slip it around the boar's head but it gets partly stuck on one tusk. Mozzo grins. He knows if he can *just* slip it the rest of the way on, he will win!

Oh no! Emilio thinks. Rosa's going to lose without even having had a turn and it's going to be *his* fault!

But in a sudden burst of strength the boar whips its head around, Mozzo falls to the ground, and the animal climbs up and over him. He holds tight onto the rope and gets dragged across the arena, only letting go when he plows face first into a pile of boar manure. The crowd erupts in laughter and the horn sounds.

Finally, it's time for Rosa. As she walks out from behind the barricades she can't believe how suddenly large the Theater seems.

The poor boar is quite done with the whole contest and runs away from Rosa. She chases the animal down and tackles it, but the boar slips out of her grip and she falls to the dirt. Now the boar looks angry. It grunts twice, shaking its head, and comes charging at Rosa full speed.

Any other kid would have been run down, but she keeps ahead of the boar. *Barely.*

"What is she *doing*?" Emilio hears someone in the crowd say. "She's running into a dead end!"

I just need to make it to those barrels! Rosa thinks, the tusks of the boar only inches from her heels.

When she gets to the barricade, she makes an amazing leap up onto a barrel. Below her, the boar crashes head first into the wood staves, cracking the barrel. Wine spills everywhere.

Rosa flips down onto the beast's back, grabs its tusks, wrestles it to the ground, and—taking the rope slung across her shoulder—ties the boar's front and hind legs together with lightning speed.

And is the **CHAMPION**!

What happens next can't be described, because it is a hundred things happening at once.

People cheering.

Boys humiliated.

Emilio and Dino hugging Rosa.

The town official pulling Rosa up onto the stage.

The Town Crier blowing his horn, trying to get the crowd to quiet down.

Now, the Order of the Golden Tusk is called to assemble.

Among its members are many Carrozzos—but not Mozzo!—as well as Amerigo Pegleg. And Rosa's father.

Father is stunned that Rosa won. His daughter! A son, he had always expected to win. But a *daughter*?

Mozzo's older brother looks absolutely sick to take off the golden sash and pin it on Rosa.

Next comes the chest. It is made of wood and painted with the outline of the head of a boar. The top comes open and reveals the trophy—the enormous curved tusk of the Calydonian Boar! It is covered with gold and sparkles in the late afternoon sun.

Only a member of the Order of the Golden Tusk may hold it, and it is the duty of the last winner to take the trophy out and hand it to the new champion. Mozzo's brother looks disgusted at the thought of doing this too, but he doesn't have to, because someone steps in front of him and says, **"No!"**

It's Father.

The crowd goes quiet.

Without saying another word, Father reaches into the trunk and picks up

the Golden Tusk himself. He walks over to Rosa with a look of dead seriousness, and holds it out for her to take.

Then he smiles.

Rosa grabs it, and holds the trophy as high in the air as she can.

Emilio has never heard anything so loud as the cheers he is hearing right now. He can't help but cheer too.

9

GLOATING IS THE HARD PART

THE next morning, the rooster crows, the sun rises, and everything is back to normal-sweet-normal.

Rosa loads up the cart as Emilio gets into the driver's seat. Dino crosses his arms as they ride off, mad that he doesn't get to make deliveries anymore and that now *he* has to start helping with the baby.

"It's not *fair!*" he calls after them as Ugo makes the turn onto the tree-lined road.

The world looks beautiful to Rosa today, and she happily gives the horns and spits as they go through the arch. "Hiya, Malefix! You dirty rotten sprite you!"

Everyone they pass on the street claps when they see Rosa, who stands in the cart and bows.

As they near Primo's, Rosa can't wait to see their cousin and gloat. After all, she didn't get a chance to at the feast last night because Primo left as soon as it started.

But when she gets to the stand, there's no Primo. Only Maria Beppina.

"Where's the *loser*?" Rosa says.

Maria Beppina shrugs.

"Ah, fiddlesticks!" Rosa says. And waits.

Finally, Primo comes up the hill, running.

"Hey, why did you leave the feast so early?" Rosa calls to him. "Did you break something? Like your pride? Haw!"

But Primo doesn't seem bothered. In fact, he's smiling like *he* is the champion.

"Is there something wrong with you?" Rosa says.

"Oh no," Primo says. "There's something right with me!" He looks around.

"You won't believe what I discovered. It's the most amazing, incredible discovery *ever*!"

"Oh yeah?" Rosa says, crossing her arms. She's mad at Primo for spoiling her fun. "I'll believe *that* when I hear it."

"What is it?" Emilio says.

Primo draws near. *"I know who the Janara lives with!"* he says, whispering. "The Janara lives with . . ." He looks around. He races away as fast as he can.

Life goes on, but our book is done!

Well, we certainly weren't expecting THAT!

Apologies to you, dear reader, for leaving you with such a cliff-hanger. I do know how you hate them.

But you have been waiting FIVE books to find out who the Janara is, so you can wait one more, can't you? We promise—in our next book, the big secret will finally be revealed!

Oh, and one OTHER thing—why is Sergio acting so strangely?

Sigismondo

RAFAELLA

BRUNO

S.   R.   B.

Life was very different in
Benevento in the 1820s.

HERE'S HOW THEY LIVED: TIME

✧ Most people never looked at a clock.

✧ If you lived near a church,
you would know what time it
was by the pattern of the
bells ringing.

✧ If you lived in the countryside, you
would tell time by looking at the sun. Its
path across the sky was divided into 12
hours in the same way a ruler is divided
into 12 inches.

✧ Instead of noon coming at 12:00, it came
  at the sixth hour, because it was when
  the sun was halfway across the sky.

✧ The hour grew or shrank depending on
  the time of year, because it was $\frac{1}{12}$th of
  however long the sun was out. So in
  Benevento, an hour in late June would
  last 75 of our minutes, while at Christ-
  mas it would last for only 46 of them.

If you want to learn MORE, please visit
witchesofbenevento.com.

HISTORICAL NOTE

THERE IS NOT NOW and—so far as I know—has never been a boar hunt celebration in Benevento. However, the myth of the Calydonian Boar does have a special place in Beneventano history. It was said that the founder of the city, Diomedes, had gifted the monster's tusks to Benevento in the aftermath of the Trojan war. According to Procopius, the tusks were still on display there at the time he was writing, in the sixth century AD. The relic disappeared at some point thereafter, but the symbol lived on in Benevento's coat of arms.

As for the hours, in the books I use the old Roman terms for them. (These live on in our own language in words like "siesta," which comes from the

Latin term "sexta," meaning the sixth hour of the day.) In the 1820s, time was in flux, with different systems being used. In the countryside, the old approach to hours as a division of daylight was still in use. In cities, the mechanical hours with 12 noon was the rule. But anywhere there was a church, much of life was regulated by bells ringing out the patterns of the church hours, which were themselves based on the Roman approach to time.

As for the Twins' father and his belief that reading was bad, this belief was certainly widespread in their day. Literacy did not become the norm in Italy until the twentieth century, and in the 1820s, it was actively discouraged. Part of this lies in the fact that the reading of the Bible by someone other than a member of the church was forbidden.

Last, I want to note that my inspiration for "Rosa of the Trees" lies in perhaps my all-time favorite book, Italo Calvino's *The Baron in the Trees*.

EMILIO'S TOP KNOTS

BOWLINE
KNOT

FIGURE EIGHT
KNOT

FISHERMAN'S
KNOT

THE BANK ROBBER'S KNOT

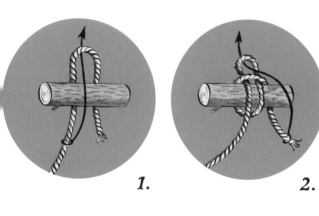

1.   **2.**

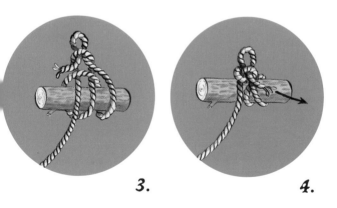

3.   **4.**

Read the other books in the

WITCHES of BENEVENTO
series!

MISCHIEF SEASON:
A Twins Story

Emilio and Rosa are tired of all the nasty tricks the Janara are playing when they ride at night making mischiefs. Maybe the fortune-teller Zia Pia will know how to stop the witches.

THE ALL-POWERFUL RING:
A Primo Story

Primo wants to prove he is the bravest, but will the ring really protect him from all danger—even from the Manalonga, who hide in wells and under bridges?

BEWARE THE CLOPPER!
A Maria Beppina Story

Maria Beppina, the timid tagalong cousin, is also the slowest runner of the five. She is always afraid that the Clopper, the old witch who chases the children, will catch her. She's also curious, so one day she decides to stop—just stop—and see what the Clopper will do.

RESPECT YOUR GHOSTS:
A Sergio Story

Sergio is in charge of Bis-Bis, the ancestor spirit who lives upstairs. Unfortunately, it's hard to satisfy all of the ghost's demands and still keep Sergio's mother happy.

JOHN BEMELMANS MARCIANO

I grew up on a farm taking care of animals. We had one spectacularly nice chicken, the Missus, who lived in a stall with an ancient horse named Gilligan, and one rooster, Leon, who pecked our heads on our way home from school. Leon, I have no doubt, was a demon. Presently I take care of two cats, one dog, and a daughter.

SOPHIE BLACKALL

I've illustrated many books for children, including the Ivy and Bean series. I drew the pictures in this book using ink made from black olives and goat spit. In 2016, I received a shiny gold Caldecott Medal for *Finding Winnie*. I grew up in Australia, but now my boyfriend and I live in Brooklyn with a cat who never moves and a bunch of children who come and go like the wind.